FORGING PASSION

A STAG GENERATIONS PREQUEL

LAINEY DAVIS

For Jenni Hermoso
#ContigoJenni

Forging Passion:
A Stag Generations Novella

By Lainey Davis
Join my newsletter and never miss a new release!
lain eydavis.com

Many thanks to Liz Alden, Liz Lincoln, Elise Kennedy, Melissa Wiesner, Nicky Lewis and Elizabeth Perry for editorial input.
Thank you for supporting independent authors!

Created with Vellum

ABOUT THIS BOOK

A one-night stand prequel to Forging Glory, a second-chance sports romance from USA Today bestselling author Lainey Davis.

I can't tear my eyes away from her.

She's incredible, the best soccer midfielder I've ever seen. Raw passion on the field.

A hundred percent my type, but a thousand percent a distraction I can't afford right now.

I've dated other athletes before. We're all too focused on our game for anything meaningful off the field. And usually, I prefer it that way.

But she's all muscle and grit, with fierce eyes that let me know she'd wreck my body. And I'd love every second.

Our connection feels immediate. The desire is mutual, like nothing I've felt before.

Then I make the mistake of a lifetime: I let her wreck my heart.

ALSO BY LAINEY DAVIS

Bridges and Bitters series

Fireball: An Enemies to Lovers Romance (Sam and AJ)

Liquid Courage: A Marriage in Crisis Romance (Chloe and Teddy)

Speed Rail: A Single Dad Romance (Piper and Cash)

Last Call: A Marriage of Convenience Romance (Esther and Koa)

Binge the following series in eBook, paperback, or audio!

Brady Family Series

Foundation: A Grouchy Geek Romance (Zack and Nicole)

Suspension: An Opposites Attract Romance (Liam and Maddie)

Inspection: A Silver Fox Romance (Kellen and Elizabeth)

Vibration: An Accidental Roommates Romance (Cal and Logan)

Current: A Secret Baby Romance (Orla and Walt)

Restoration: A Silver Fox Redemption Romance (Mick and Celeste)

Oak Creek Series

The Nerd and the Neighbor (Hunter and Abigail)

The Botanist and the Billionaire (Diana and Asa)

The Midwife and the Money (Archer and Opal)

The Planner and the Player (Fletcher and Thistle)

Stag Brothers Series

Sweet Distraction (Tim and Alice)

Filled Potential (Ty and Juniper)

Fragile Illusion (Thatcher and Emma)

A Stag Family Christmas

Beautiful Game (Hawk and Lucy)

Stag Generations Series

Forging Passion (Wes and Cara prequel)

Forging Glory (Wes and Cara)

Forging Legacy (coming soon)

Forging Chaos (coming soon)

Stone Creek University

Deep in the Pocket: A Football Romance

Hard Edge: A Hockey Romance

Possession: A Football Romance

CONTENT NOTE

This book contains inappropriate and harassing behavior from a male character in a position of power. While his actions are not described in graphic detail, some readers may find the dynamics disturbing or uncomfortable. Please read with discretion.

The author in no way condones this type of conduct. The character's behavior represents an unfortunate reality for many women and people of marginalized genders. His characterization aims to bring awareness to systemic issues in sports culture and society as a whole.

While the depicted events are fictional, their impact is very real. If you find this content too upsetting, you may want to pass on this title. Please take care of yourself.

CHAPTER 1
WES

I FLASH my ID to the airport security and kick off my shower slides, sticking them alongside my phone in one of those gray tubs before I hoist my bag onto the belt. This isn't my first time traveling for soccer and I know better than to let my gear out of sight. No way in hell will I be breaking in emergency cleats from a box store near the airport.

I step through the metal detector, and no sooner do I grab my phone from the belt when I hear it buzzing and see the rapid, incoming messages.

DAD:

Where are you?

DAD:

Seriously, Wes. Enough. Where are you?

DAD:

Do you want to give your mother a seizure? Pick up the phone, son.

That last message is specifically designed to guilt me, but I'm not falling for it. Mom's epilepsy has been stable for years and Dad can fuck off.

I recognize that leaving school with only one year to go seems like a foolish choice, but if I want to get serious about playing pro soccer, about playing for the national team someday, then I need to focus on my game.

Sure, it's messed up that academics are the distraction in my student-athlete world, but it's the truth. I'm putting in at least 20 hours a week of practice, conditioning, weight training, and watching film. I'm studying the game so much I literally have nothing left in the tank when it's time to hit the books.

So yeah. I skipped out. At least, I can see how my dad views it that way. I let my college coach know about my plans to step down. I actually filed the papers to withdraw from school, too. I'm officially unaffiliated with the university. As of tomorrow, I'm a free agent, ready to show off my game to all the scouts at the elite open-invitation camp in California.

Technically, it's a camp for the U.S. national team coaches to look at potential players leading up to the Olympics, but I know I'm not ready for that milestone. I'm there to get picked up by a pro team hoping to round out their roster with fresh legs and healthy knees. Mid-season, long after the draft, these teams have ditched the guys who couldn't cut it or snapped their ligaments. Scouts swarm these camps with contracts at the ready.

Do I want to piss off my family? Do I want to ditch my cousin, who's been my roommate and teammate for years? Of course not. But Wyatt's on his own path, and I need to do what's right for me. At least he's not irate about it like my dad. Although, to be fair, Wyatt knows where I am right now, and my dad is apparently having a stroke because he thinks I'm missing.

Thatcher Stag can't stand not knowing where his family is every second of the day. I know he's overcome some abandonment trauma, but seriously, no parent needs to keep "find my phone" tracking on his 21-year-old son.

I grit my teeth and fire off a text to my mom, promising her that I'm just fine, that I know what I'm doing, and that I'll be in California for a few days. I'd have thought with two brothers as professional athletes, my dad would understand a lot more about seizing opportunities while my body is fresh, but he's too focused on me keeping non-soccer options open that he can't see it's costing me opportunities on the field.

I'm seizing the day, damn it.

I enrolled in this open camp, and committed to a year in the championship circuit playing semi-pro if things don't work out for me this weekend. Where will I land? I have absolutely no idea. It could be London, Chicago, Miami…that's the beautiful thing about the beautiful game. It's truly global and as long as I'm willing to live out of a suitcase—which I totally am—the opportunities are mine to pass up. And I'm done passing this particular ball. Wyatt and I have the lease on our apartment until the end of the month, so I have plenty of time to figure out where to stash my belongings.

But if I have anything to say about it, I'll know everything I need by the end of this weekend when the pro soccer coaches are fighting each other to pull me off their discovery lists.

• • •

I shove my phone back in my sweats and grab my duffel from the security belt, looking around for my slides. An irritated female voice hollers at me. "Hey, that's my bag, asshole."

I whip my head around to find a barefoot Latina woman glaring at me, toned arms crossed over her chest as her red-tipped toes dig into the tile floor. She looks murderously angry, dark hair in a braid over one shoulder, dark eyes glaring out from above tawny cheeks flushed with frustration. She is exactly the kind of woman I'd chase if I had the time and energy for such things.

But I don't, I remind myself quickly. She moves her hands to her hips, causing her t-shirt to stretch across her chest. It reads OU SOCCER. My breath rushes out of my body. The temptation is extreme—I love athletic women. I love joking around with them and I love the feel of their bodies against mine. And sexiest of all, this one is annoyed with me. "You have my bag."

I look down at my duffel and see that it is, in fact, not mine. There are no scuffs on it, for starters, and it's got the name MORENO embroidered on the side instead of STAG. "My bad," I say, slipping the bag off my shoulder and handing it to her. She snatches it with a huff and looks past me, I assume searching for her shoes.

Which seem to be caught up in a line at the machine, where the security agent is scowling at my actual soccer bag. The angry woman sniffs. "What did you do? Leave your tape scissors in there?"

"Shit." My stomach lurches because I definitely did leave my athletic tape scissors in the side pocket of my bag. I look around for someone to explain, but they're already beckoning me toward a podium. I can tell they'll be wagging a blue-gloved finger at me for my error.

I pad over there in my socks–my slides are still somewhere on the belt—and explain about the scissors. "I understand that you have to take them," I tell the guy, who rolls his eyes so hard I can almost hear it.

"This is serious, sir. You can't bring weapons onto a plane."

"Yes, I understand that. Like I said. I'm sorry."

He tosses the scissors into a bin next to the podium and gives my bag a final rummage, wrinkling his nose at the pungent odor from my shin guards. "Please make sure to take all your belongings from the belt," he says, shoving the bag in my direction. I nod and grab my stuff so I can hustle to my gate.

The flight is half boarded by the time I get there and as I make my way to my seat, I can't help the grin that splits my face. Moreno is sitting in the seat next to mine.

CHAPTER 2
CARA

I'M TRYING NOT to stress. It's not going well. I was just a total bitch to a guy in the security line because he picked up my bag by accident. Gah. But I basically have everything riding on this weekend and I have no filter right now.

Which is why I have a whole string of apology messages to send to my roommates back at school for rushing out of our apartment in a huff to catch my flight. I could have had a ride from Shante if I was capable of accepting help from anyone. I could have gotten here much earlier, and not had to sprint from the shuttle bus only to get stuck in the security line behind a guy who is far too attractive for his own good.

"Nope," I say as I fill my water bottle from the fountain near my gate. "Not looking at men right now, attractive or otherwise."

I took a two-hour bus from my college in Ohio, followed by a city bus and an airport shuttle, and that's only today's part of my journey. I've been on this path to this training camp my entire life, from the first time I laced up a pair of cleats. No—from the moment I watched women like Brandy Chastain and Megan Rapinoe slay on the pitch and begged my parents to *buy* me a pair of cleats.

All the hours in the weight room these past four years, all the conditioning, all the physical therapy for sprained ligaments…it all comes down to this moment.

They announce boarding for my flight, and I make my way onto the plane, tossing my duffel bag into the overhead compartment before settling into my seat. Since I'm still allowed to use my phone, I decide it's time to eat some humble pie and I text my roommates.

MIDFIELD MAMIS

Made it to the plane!

SHANTE:

Oh, she's talking to us now.

TONI:

Probably forgot something she wants us to bring her real quick.

I'm so sorry I was a total bitch this morning. I'm so nervous, guys.

TONI:

We know, girl. You're going to be great. Don't even worry about it.

SHANTE:

Toni, you know she's worried.

I mean, I wasn't gonna say anything snippy. But yeah, I'm a wreck.

SHANTE:

And?

And I love you, and you're the best teammates and the best roommates and I'll tell you everything as soon as I get back.

ROSALIE:

We know you're going to kill it and we already planned a carbo load for Monday.

SHANTE:

Since when are we eating wheat?

ROASLIE:

I mean, maybe it's zoodles and meatballs.

TONI:

Zoodles are NOT pasta. I don't like pretending. And we don't have to follow a nutrition plan anymore. Except for Cara. <3

Okay, well, I'll eat whatever I can with you, and I'll love it.

SHANTE:

Love you!

ROSLIE:

[heart emoji. Soccer ball emoji. Trophy emoji]

The flight attendant starts telling people to put our phones away, so I slide mine in my pants pocket just as the last passenger hustles on to the plane.

I look up and of course it's that white dude from security, whose giant duffel no longer fits in the overhead compartments because they're all full. I watch his muscles move inside his t-shirt as he hoists up the lids to nearby bins, then pulls them back down. His ass is right at my eye level and, not gonna lie, I stare. He's got a perfect bubble butt accentuated by his gray sweats and I suck in a breath, wondering if he will turn to face me and try the bins on my side of the aisle, because then I'll really get an eyeful.

Even if he didn't have a soccer bag with tape scissors, I would have spotted him as someone in training. That level of arm muscle doesn't just show up on a guy.

I do like to appreciate athletes. One thing that's true about all of us, we work our bodies to the limit, and we look damn good. I've had my share of adventures on tournament weekends. There's a pretty standard rule that my soccer teammates don't sleep around with the men's team, or even the men's teams for other sports at our school. Too much risk for distraction and drama, even if there's a smaller number of female collegiate athletes who are interested in men to begin with.

"Aha! Got it." The guy slams the bin shut with a grin and looks around, almost like he's expecting back pats. He brushes his shaggy brown hair back from his forehead with one hand and looks up and down the plane. I spy the one remaining empty seat on this plane: right next to me, and I groan as he sinks into his seat.

The flight attendants walk through the aisle for the safety demonstration, and I notice that both the male and female crew pause to smile at the sweatpants guy. A woman wearing the demonstration life vest stops in the aisle and beams at him, touching his arm. "Remember, anyone can blow the tube to inflate." She inserts the red plastic between her pursed crimson lips and winks before continuing down the aisle.

He smirks. "I notice she didn't offer you a personal safety demonstration." Is he talking to me?

I look over at him and he's got his brows raised, fingers tapping on his long legs, one of which spreads way into the aisle and the other is smashed against the seat in front of him. "How do you know I didn't get my one-on-one before you got onto the plane? You were awfully late…"

He grins. "I'd say I was right on time." At least that leg isn't pressing against mine.

"You going to follow her to the back of the plane for a snack?" I reach up and twist the air vent to full blast as the plane starts to taxi. He chuckles.

"I better stick close by in case you need rescuing. I have, after all, had some advanced coaching."

A puff of laughter escapes my lips before I can think of a retort. I like this sort of flirting because it keeps my mind off the pressure of this try-out camp.

He tips a chin in my direction. "Soccer, huh? OU? Me, too." I arch a brow at him. "I mean, not at OU obviously. You going to the camp in Cali?"

"I am. You, too?"

He nods. "I am."

I exhale. "So, your guts are twisted, too?" I wince. Maybe he's totally confident. Hell, for all I know he's already capped for the national team. I don't follow the men's game at all. But I'm relieved when his face softens, and he nods.

"Oh, I'm a total wreck." He twists to offer me his hand to shake. "Wes Stag, striker."

I grip his hand, feeling a flutter in my belly at the warm, firm contact. "Cara Moreno. Midfield."

"I hate midfield," he laughs. "It's exhausting."

"Hmm. Maybe try upping your fitness routine." We both laugh and then grip our respective arm rests as the plane jolts off the ground. Our forearms are pressed together on the arm rest between us, and I focus on that as we hit the sky. My phone flies from my pocket and skitters into the aisle and Wes reaches to pick it up.

He holds it out to me, and I slide it from his hand. His middle finger lingers, sliding down my palm and making me shiver. "We should get dinner or something when we land. My agenda doesn't start until morning."

I press my lips together, considering. I really need to network on this trip, and I'll have a roommate at the hotel anyway. But there's no harm in a meal before I check in, right? In the silence, Wes raises his brows, expectantly. He's gorgeous and funny, and he knows about soccer. High level soccer.

I can't shake the feeling it would be a mistake to turn him down.

But I also worry it's a mistake to say yes.

CHAPTER 3
WES

"WE'LL SEE," Cara says, toying with the end of her braid and then tugging on her tray table. I envy the way she has enough space to pull it all the way flat. My legs are way too long to even consider it. My knees get smashed every time the guy in front of me adjusts his weight. But squashed up close to a beautiful, sassy soccer player, I don't mind as much. Hopefully she can distract me from the spasms I'll probably get in my back from folding my body like a crouching insect.

"Well, Cara Moreno, you have to at least promise to sit next to me on the shuttle to the hotel. Wait. Does the women's team stay in the same hotel as the men's for this thing? Do they want to risk everyone ... canoodling?"

I realize too late that I've revealed myself to be a first timer at this elite camp, but Cara seems unfazed. She turns her body slightly so she's almost facing me in the cramped space. I can smell her, fresh powder and floral soap. I want to bury my face in that braid and inhale. "Not sure how you don't already know this about women's soccer, Stag, but there's usually plenty of same-gender canoodling regardless." She laughs, and I realize I'm hanging on to some really outdated assumptions. Cara bites her lip and says, "I'm at the Summit."

I nod. "Same. So, about that shuttle ride…"

* * *

We flirt the entire flight, joking about the agenda, realizing the men's and women's teams share some staff members. I'm careful not to mention my relation to the coaching staff of my hometown teams. I'm not sure why I don't tell Cara that fitness coach Lucy Moyer is my aunt, or that my uncle coaches the professional men's soccer team in Pittsburgh. Cara seems blissfully unaware of my family, and I realize it's a relief. I spend enough time worried that people think my relatives pulled strings to get me where I am.

Maybe they did back in high school and maybe they did to get me seen by the college scouts. But I'm pretty confident that I made my way here today on my own merit. My college coach sure didn't make any calls on my behalf after I quit the team.

Cara flops her head back against the seat and sighs. "I have so much riding on this weekend. You know?"

"Trust me. I get it."

She turns her head to stare at me, her dark eyes intense, like she can see right inside my head. "How can you stand it? The pressure? Sometimes I feel like, if I am this messed up about the possibility of making the national team, maybe I'm not cut out to wear that jersey anyway."

I shake my head and place my hand on hers on the arm rest. She doesn't pull her arm back or flinch, so I keep it there. "Don't think like that. Anyone would be a mess going into this camp. Even the veterans. It's not like their spot on the roster is etched in stone. It's a big deal to put yourself out there and risk being told you don't have what it takes."

She smiles. "It feels good to meet someone who gets that."

"Same, Cara. Same." I tap my other palm on my thigh, realizing my right leg is almost touching hers. How are these planes so small? The warmth of her body radiates into me, despite the blast of air she's got blowing from her vent. "I'll let you in on a secret." I can't believe I'm about to speak all this out loud, but what do I have to lose? She's on the same path. She doesn't know my history, but if she's trying out for the national team, she knows something about what my life has looked like on the pitch. "I don't even expect to get called to the Stars and Stripes. I'm here to get seen by the pro scouts."

Cara's smile lights up her entire face and she tucks a few tendrils of loose hair behind her ears. "Wes," she whispers. "Same!"

When we land, Cara and I grab our duffel bags—each of us with the proper bag this time—and she does agree to ride the shuttle with me to the hotel. But I can tell her head is already into her purpose for being here. Tonight isn't the night to let loose. Cara mutters to herself on the shuttle bus and I fight back the urge to squeeze her knee, to reassure her that she'll be great tomorrow. I have no idea how she'll play. How she'll respond to the pressure of being scrutinized. But something tells me she will rise to this occasion and shine above the other players.

As we pull up to the hotel there's a huge crowd of soccer players sprawled all through the lobby, with some chaos as people try to get checked into their rooms. I see a bunch of familiar faces and I hear a woman with a clipboard calling Cara's name from over near the vending machine.

She waves and holds up a finger, turning toward me. "So."

I slide my hands in my pockets. "So."

Cara rolls her eyes and pulls out her phone. "You should give me your number. You know, in case I have questions about life vests or something."

I grin. "You want instructions for how to blow a tube?"

Cara doesn't blush and she doesn't back away. She thrusts the phone toward me. "By Saturday night, I'll be ready for some turbulence."

I enter my number into her phone and then call myself, silencing the phone with one hand as I pass back hers. But I don't let go right away, stroking her hand with my thumb instead. I like that this has become a thing with us already. "I'll help you assume the brace position, Cara." I wink at her.

She smiles a tight-lipped half-grin and hoists her bag higher on her shoulder. I watch her walk away toward her competition, admiring the rear view as she leaves.

And then I turn to face the guys I've played against for years in college, the guys who are even bigger rivals this weekend than ever before. Time to get my head in the game.

CHAPTER 4
CARA

AS A DIVISION ONE ATHLETE, I've gotten used to some pretty swanky accommodations for soccer functions, and this training center is no different. The hotel is super clean and spacious, with all-white linens that I'm scared I'll get muddy later when I'm covered in grass and dirt from the field.

I'm rooming with a white woman named Jay, who played keeper for Seattle. I've played against her before, but never really got to know her. When we get to our room, we toss our bags on the ground and look at one another, hesitant.

She runs a tattooed hand through her short, straight hair and sighs. "I really don't like sleeping next to the vent thingy. Is that okay?"

I sigh right back in relief. "I really prefer sleeping further from the door! This is great."

We spend some time unpacking, swapping small talk to break the awkwardness. We both just graduated and have our sights set on the pros, with the national team as a "someday" goal.

"They're taking younger and younger players, though," Jay says, pursing her lips as she lays out her goalie kits on the dresser. "Maybe I've already missed my window. I don't know."

"Well, I worry about the same things, but I'm sure the competition is tighter for keeper since there's only one of you." She's got an array of pale blue, black, and lime green outfits. "Do you have to bring all of them with you all weekend in case we scrimmage?"

She shakes her head. "Nah. I just wanted to be ready."

We both like to fall asleep to white noise and we turn in pretty early to help combat the jet lag, but not until we chug water with electrolyte tablets stirred in. Jay cranks the volume on a sleep sounds app on her phone and we snap off the lights. And then my brain goes haywire, running through all the skills I know I need to perfect, all the flaws I can't unsee after the last round of film I watched with my college coach.

I can't do this all night and I silently chide myself for obsessing. But if I stop thinking about soccer, that only leaves thoughts of Wes. It's seriously unfair for someone to be that good looking. He's the total package: funny, tall, fit, and confident. I don't regret skipping dinner with him tonight since both of us really do need to concentrate. But I can't help fantasizing about what it will be like if we really do sneak away from the crowd after the last session ends on Saturday.

Will he really help me take the edge off? Unwind and

forget the stress and pressure for a few minutes? Maybe it'll actually last longer than a few minutes with Wes. Or maybe we'll both be too exhausted to copulate after 16 hours of intense, high-level soccer.

Jay and I sit together on the shuttle bus to the training center. Apparently, the men and women are training in a different area of the facility, which makes sense since we need all the space in the locker rooms and offices.

"Wow." Jay and I stop in the tunnel to the field, looking out on the perfect grass in the California sunshine.

"Yeah," I tell her. "Wow." I know we've each experienced some pretty big stadiums, but this is beyond. This is the home of pro soccer for men and women, a stadium that regularly sells out with 20,000 tickets. "This is where it all happens."

"Damn right." Jay claps me on the back. "You got this, Moreno."

I punch her in the upper arm. "You got this, too."

Every woman in this locker room is the best of the best on their university team full of elite players. Or, I realize, the best of their professional club team. I try not to gawk at the group of women along one side of the locker room because I've definitely waited in line for each of their autographs in the past.

"Jay," I whisper. "We are in the same locker room with—"

"Don't be weird, Moreno." Her eyes widen and she

shakes her head. "They're trying out this weekend, same as us. Right? All of us earned the right to be here."

"I wish I had your confidence about it," I mutter. I think back on the summer I spent living at school instead of going home. My parents were sad about it, but I wanted to graduate in August and focus on my game, rather than tack on one more semester. I clocked 30 hours a week on individual skill work with our positional coaches. I lifted weights until my thighs busted out of my jeans.

Jay's right. I can't afford to fuck this up by forgetting that I'm a bad ass.

I also can't forget the reward I've set up for myself at the end of the weekend…

CHAPTER 5
WES

THIS MORNING'S sessions were brutal, and I loved every second. Every guy here is better than the best guys on my university team, and I've been keeping up just fine. I know I'm right where I belong, and when we get a break to hydrate, I wander over to the fence with my sports drink, leaning back and just taking in the scene.

The women are using the field inside the stadium this morning while the men train on one of the practice fields, and we're switching this afternoon. But from this angle I can see through the stadium gates onto the field and the women are scrimmaging.

I chug the rest of my drink and walk a bit closer, trying to see.

A streak of red catches my eye and I stare at the best midfielder I've ever seen. She's got MORENO on jersey back in white letters.

Cara's braid flies behind her as she attacks up the sideline, two defenders on her back and ready to pounce. I watch, mesmerized, as she plants a foot and weaves right, the ball following along like it's an extension of her cleats.

Her movements are graceful and devastating as she darts into gaps that shouldn't be wide enough. Cara makes it all seem effortless, pulling the ball back with one toe and changing direction to hug the sideline. As she approaches the goal, I can see she has the keeper beat. She's got a clear shot and it's going to smash into the back of the net.

Except she doesn't strike. She fakes right and sends a sweet pass to a teammate, who toes the ball into the center of the goal. "Fuck," I whisper. Now that was a boss move. The coaches watching the session take notes and I see one of them whip out a phone, tapping frantically on the screen.

It shouldn't be this hot. She's not trying to be sexual right now. But I'm hard as a goal post watching her move. Honestly, I think I drool a little bit, but I pretend it's sweat and wipe my face with my jersey as I hear my name being called.

I indulge in one more glance as Cara's teammates swarm around her for hugs and high-fives. She's sort of shy about what just happened, her full, pouty lips tipped in a small smile.

"Stag! Let's move!"

I jog toward the sound of the coach's voice, ready for my own scrimmage and my own chance to show off my skills in a game scenario. As the striker coach pulls me and the other guys in to talk strategy, I marvel at just how specialized the training is at the next level of soccer. Even though I played D1 in college, we had all generalized coaches except for the goalies.

I'm spending this entire weekend not only showing these coaches what I can do, but also learning from them. I'm guessing the men's and women's staff have some of the same training plans because Coach Bev tells us the objective is to move the ball along the sideline and pass toward the center for the shots on goal.

It's easy to see why some guys would want to be glory hogs for a camp like this, to score and put points on the board. But I commit to showing Bev and the other staff that I can follow instructions and adapt to the gameplan.

On the pitch, I feel a little like Cara, moving the ball well, outwitting defenders. When I do see a shot on goal from the right corner, it's hard as hell not to take it, but as soon as I pass to another guy from my row, I can hear Coach Bev bellowing in delight.

Soon after, an air horn sounds, signaling our lunch break, and everyone makes their way to the locker rooms. I take my time on the walk over, feeling damn good about my morning, and Coach Bev shouts my name.

"Stag! Looking good out there. This your first open camp with us?"

I nod and she elbows a man standing next to her. I know Bev isn't on the national team staff, but I recognize her companion as the president of Soccer USA. "Lou, keep an eye on this one, hey? You'll be hearing his name in a few years."

Lou holds out a hand, smiling. "Lou Rubeo. And what name should I be looking for?"

"Wes Stag, sir." I shake his hand and he pats my upper arm.

"Stag. I'll keep that in mind." He raises his brows and walks in a different direction as Bev falls in step beside me.

"Don't mind him. Or do. But I've got you on my list, kid."

Now it's my turn to lift my brows. "What list might that be?"

She waves a hand. "It's a mental list for now. But I'm going to make sure you're in for the exhibition match tomorrow. I want you to be seen, okay?"

I nod rapidly. "Thank you. I want to do my best out there." She smiles and pats my upper arm, shooing me toward the locker room.

I strip out of my cleats and socks and into shower slides, feeling like a million bucks even as I make my way to the training room to get help stretching my lower back. Everything seems to be falling into place. I'm not usually superstitious. I don't keep the same socks all season or give up shaving during playoffs or anything like that. But I can't help but wonder if Cara Moreno is my lucky charm.

CHAPTER 6
CARA

"YOU SAUCY MINX!" Jay claps me on the back after our morning scrimmage ends. "I thought you were going to score right between my legs, but you fired off that pass. So great."

I laugh, still high on the endorphin rush of perfecting the strategy the coaches asked for. "Thanks. I bet you would have blocked it if I took the shot. But we were working on that decoy move."

Jay shakes her head. "Well, it freaking worked. You grabbing lunch?"

"Yeah, I just have to change shoes quick."

"Cool. I'm grabbing a bag of ice for my shoulder. Meet you up there?"

I nod and she clacks off toward the training room, still wearing her cleats and today's bright orange goalie kit.

I'm still shaking with happiness at how I played this morning. I don't know if it's the sunshine or the atmosphere or if I just click with this group of players, but I can objectively say I'm kicking ass at this camp. I walk slowly toward the locker room, taking my time and basking in satisfaction, and I hear footsteps as someone approaches.

"Hello, there."

I turn and see a guy in a Soccer USA polo. He steps closer and I realize it's not just any guy, but the president of the whole organization. I recognize him from television when I've seen the national team play. "Oh. Hi."

He smiles and his eyes dip to my chest. "You looked pretty good out there. What's your name?"

"Uh, Cara. Cara Moreno."

"Nice to meet you, Cara. I'm Lou." He holds out his hand, and when I shake it, he doesn't let go as soon as I expect him to.

Cold dread snakes up my spine, like someone dumped a bucket of ice over my head. His smile creeps me out more than the handshake. Maybe because this guy is really important when it comes to the national team? I decide it must be my nerves and I pull my hand back, placing it on my duffel bag and holding it tight against my side.

"Well, I've got my eye on you, Cara. Hope to see a lot more of you."

I'm about to stutter out a thanks when Jay rounds the corner with the ice. She glares at Lou, who looks up at her and immediately backs up a few inches. Jay tips her chin. "We should get up to lunch, Cara."

I nod. "Yeah. I'm starved."

Lou smiles, but it's a false smile, even creepier than when he held my hand in his. "You ladies enjoy your meal."

I mutter another thanks and Jay says nothing at all as Lou walks away, whistling.

"You okay?" Jay is stern and serious, and I worry she thinks something bad happened.

"Oh, yes. Totally. I think I'm just exhausted." My hands are shaking a little as the adrenaline wears off from earlier.

She nods, her face still apprehensive. "Well, let's get some protein."

We make our way to the cafeteria and pile our plates with chicken breasts and sweet potatoes. By the time we've each had a few mouthfuls, we're laughing alongside the other people at our table as they verbally rehash the morning's cardio activities.

"Let's just skip as high as we can for a mile and a half," Jay jokes. "Really test out the strength of our sports bras before we scrimmage."

Everyone laughs until our sides ache and I'm back to feeling great. I'm sure I was overreacting to how Lou from Soccer USA made me feel and I chalk the experience up to hunger and adrenaline from the scrimmage. The afternoon session goes amazing just like the morning, even if I am utterly exhausted by the end. I decide to skip the shower at the stadium. I'll wait until I'm back at the hotel when I can take my time with a bottle of tea tree conditioner, so I check my messages while I wait for the shuttle bus.

My group chat with my roommates is full of good luck notes, videos of professional players scoring goals and celebrating, and then a picture of my entire college team after a workout. Every one of my teammates wishes me the best, even the ones I just graduated with who didn't make the cut for the open camp.

I'm still choked up and emotional when I get out of my shower, but Jay is fired up, bouncing around the room in a swimsuit. "There you are! Come on, everyone is doing hydration recovery." I furrow my brow in confusion, and she shakes her head. "We're invading the hotel pool. Grab your suit."

I laugh at myself. "For a minute I worried I forgot an active cool-down session or something."

Jay tosses me a towel from the bathroom. "No, we're just going rogue and enjoying some sunshine. Some of us live in Seattle, where we never see that yellow guy up there."

I quickly slip into my two-piece. It's not the sexiest bathing suit from my drawer—it's the functional one I use for ice baths, so the top has a lot of coverage, and the bottom is more boy shorts than bikini. "Okay, ready." I toss a long t-shirt over my head and shove my feet back in my shower slides.

The two of us head down to the hotel pool and find the entire space is crawling with soccer players. Jay whistles. "That is one fine display."

I nod, staring at the corner of the deck where a group of men are shedding shirts. "Mmm, yes." I look over to Jay and see she's got the same expression on her face as she stares at a group of women in two-piece suits similar to mine. We laugh at one another and drop our towels on the nearest lounge chair.

"Too bad we have to stay focused." Jay sighs.

"No harm in looking though, right?" I slide into the pool, the heated water a delicious surprise. "Oh my god, this feels amazing." I say it to Jay but when I lean my head back in the water and then right myself and open my eyes, I see that she's swum off toward the deep end and Wes Stag is looming over me from the pool deck.

"It looks amazing," he drawls as he drops to sit on the edge, dangling his legs into the water.

I smooth my hair back from my face and stretch my neck. Wes Stag without a shirt is entirely unfair when I'm trying to keep my head in the soccer game. But then again, if I let my brain rest and destress for a bit, maybe I'll be sharper tomorrow.

"Wait," Wes says. "Were you talking about yourself or the pool?"

Do I have the energy for this level of flirting after a hard day of soccer? "You should get in and research that question," I tell him. *Yes. Yes I do have the energy for this.*

Taking the invitation, Wes slides into the water and submerges fully, coming to stand and shaking the water off his golden muscles. I lean close, trying to make out the tattoo he has on his chest. "Oh," I smile. "A stag. I get it."

He traces the tattoo absentmindedly. "It's kind of a family thing. The laurel branches are for my grandma."

"So, everyone has the same tat? That's pretty cool."

He nods, running his hands along the surface of the water, not making any bones about checking me out. So I drink my fill and stare right back. I mutter, "if all the guys have the tattoo on your chest, where do the women get it done?"

He winks. "You'll have to become a Stag woman and find out, won't you?"

"Oh really? How does one become a Stag woman." I back away from him in the water and he follows, both of us squatting low so we're fully submerged up to the neck. "I'm a try-before-I-buy kind of gal…"

I like how I feel when I'm with him, confident, flirty, like I can say anything I want, and he wants to hear it. I can be up front in my interest in boning him and he clearly feels the same way. It's refreshing. It's thrilling.

He reaches out to touch my shoulder and I welcome the contact. My body leans back against his touch almost instinctively. It feels so different from when that Lou guy was near me in the hall earlier. I shudder, chasing thoughts of him away and focusing on Wes and his finger tracing my shoulder blade.

"It would look good on you here," he says, palm skating along my bare shoulder blade. "But it would also look hot on your upper arm." He moves his hand to the dip of my bicep.

This thing between us is electric. I know if I looked down, I'd find him at least half hard and I resist swimming to him, pressing against all that magnetic heat and muscle. The universe put him in my path at that airport, sat him right next to me, and now gifted me the chance to see Wes Stag all wet and warm in this pool.

I close my eyes. We still have a big day tomorrow and I cannot let myself slip away for a quickie with so much on the line.

I exhale through pursed lips and back away from him a few inches, leaning my back on the edge of the pool. He slides up beside me and I turn to face him. "Tell me about your family. Where are you from?"

"I'm a Pittsburgh boy, born and raised. My entire family is there." He looks up, pondering. "Well, some of my cousins are away at college. There are a lot of us all in school at once." He chuckles. "Our dads sometimes curse their choice to all having kids at about the same time."

I smile. "I have a big extended family, too. Mexican Catholics and all that."

"Extended family—not a lot of siblings?"

I let my toes float up out of the pool, noticing that the polish is chipped on one of my big toes. Probably where a striker stepped on me earlier today. It'll hurt later. "I'm an only child. My parents got divorced when I was young and neither of them had any more kids." I shrug. "They get along okay."

We talk about my upbringing in Ohio, how I suffered through over a decade of Catholic girls' schools. "My parents would have sent me to an all-girls' college, too, if I hadn't gotten a scholarship to OU."

"Thank god for Title IX, then, I guess." Wes taps his hand on the concrete pool deck.

"You know about Title IX?"

He scoffs. "Everyone knows about Title IX. Or…I guess everyone in my family. Do people usually not know?"

Wes seems taken aback as I explain how many people in Ohio have never heard of women's soccer, even in this day and age, and how many people are surprised I earned a free college degree playing soccer and expect to play professionally.

His eyes widen at that. "Man, my one aunt is an Olympian and some sort of high-powered court judge. She got involved in getting the US women's hockey team equal pay."

"Holy shit, really?" As he talks, I learn that passionate feminism is now my biggest turn-on in a guy. He keeps going.

"And another aunt coaches professional soccer—men and women. I guess in my family we just talk a lot more about those sorts of equity issues."

"That's amazing." I nudge closer to him. I want to tell

him that I'd like to meet his family, to see this group of people who teach their sons about gender equity. But I'm not here looking for love. I intend to be a woman who is paid to play pro soccer, and I've spent decades convincing my parents that such a thing is possible.

This thing between us is totally happening—it'll be hot and fast. The gravy on the feast of this weekend. I chew the inside of my cheek and look at him, reminding myself that all bets are off the second tomorrow's afternoon session ends.

Jay shouts my name and waves a towel. "We're grabbing dinner. You in?"

I nod and turn to Wes. "That's my cue."

"Until tomorrow, Moreno."

I can't tell which is the more impressive feat: acing that plan on the field today, or walking away from a very wet, half-naked Wes Stag.

CHAPTER 7
WES

I WATCH Cara climb out of the pool, the sun glinting off the muscles on her back and shoulders. She walks away with her friend, drying herself off with the too-small hotel towel. There shouldn't really be anything sexy about a woman dabbing pool water off her neck, but I'm fully erect in the shallow end as she clacks away in her shower slides.

Under normal circumstances, I'd have her against the wall by now, our tongues tangling. But she's right—we've both got a lot riding on this weekend. I guess the anticipation adds to the intrigue, too. By tomorrow night we'll both be amped up and ready to unleash our inner beasts.

I splash water on my face and pat my own hungry stomach, wondering when the guys will head into the cafeteria for dinner.

Someone has to start that party train and climb out of the pool. I make my way over to the chair with my stuff and almost bump into a woman hustling into the fenced-in space. "Woah, there," she says, gripping my arm with a strong hand. And then she looks up to see my face. "Wesley Stag? I wondered when I'd see your mug."

"Aunt Lucy?"

My aunt swats at my arm with her clipboard. "Stay right there, mister. I need to give my card to a prospect and then you and I are having a chat."

I dry my hair and slip into my t-shirt as I watch her continue hustling with one of the women's players at the far end of the pool. Aunt Lucy pulls a card from her fanny pack and gestures excitedly as the player beams. I didn't think individual team fitness coaches would be at one of these camps recruiting, but I guess the Pittsburgh Hot Metal sent a deep bench to scout talent.

Lucy smiles at her prospect, shakes her hand, and then my aunt whips her entire body back to me, her face shifting to a stern scowl. She kicks a recliner toward me and sinks onto another one. "Sit." I do. "Wes. Your father is beside himself. Your uncles had to take him running and rough him up so he'd calm down. You want to tell me when the hell this family started keeping secrets and making huge decisions that leave other Stags in the dark?"

I sigh and lean forward, my elbows on my tired thighs. "Aunt Lucy, if I gave my parents advance notice I wasn't finishing school, they'd overstep. They'd go to the bursar and pre-pay tuition. You've met my dad. He's stubborn as hell."

"Oh, trust me, I'm familiar with the Stag man form of stubbornness." Aunt Lucy rolls her eyes. She's married to my Uncle Hawk, who only found out about his brothers as an adult when he was transferred to Pittsburgh's pro soccer team. I was about six years old when my family learned there was a fourth Stag brother…who happens to have a different last name from the rest of us. They've had a lot of years to make up for lost time, though. My extended family is insanely close.

Aunt Lucy leans forward and looks me in the eye, grabbing hold of my chin. "You could have at least talked to me and Hawk about your plans to go pro right away. You know we would have given you advice. Made introductions…"

Her voice drifts off as I shake my head out of her hand. "I don't want handouts because of my family. I want to sign with a team because I'm the fucking best player for the roster." She breathes in and out through her nose a few times, her hands tapping her clipboard. A thought occurs to me. "Uncle Hawk isn't here this weekend, is he?"

I can't help the flinch my face betrays at the idea of my uncle activating the family group chat from the bleachers. I'm sure he and Aunt Lucy are less than thrilled that I swore their son to secrecy regarding my plans. Honestly, I'm impressed Wyatt sat on this news and I definitely owe him big time.

"No, Wes, your uncle is home prepping the Forge for the playoffs while half his starters are here trying out for the national team."

I nod, because I assumed she'd be back doing the same thing with the women's team—half the reason I chose this particular camp to take my shot. I knew word would get back to everyone eventually. I just wanted to go into the inevitable hard conversations having made my mark. I'm assuming I will leave here tomorrow with offers. I've bet my whole future on it.

I scratch the back of my neck and make a face of contrition at my aunt. "So…why are *you* here, then?"

"Gah." She runs her hands down her khaki shorts and leans forward. "I got an urgent text about a keeper, a midfielder, and an unbelievable striker that our rivals in Louisville are planning to woo." She shimmies her shoulders. "I made myself available for the last-minute first-class direct flight out here."

I laugh, imagining her sprinting from the stadium in Pittsburgh to the airport in her polo shirt and fanny pack. She'd probably get there faster than if she drove, half because the traffic there sucks and half because my Aunt Lucy is fit as fuck from so many years training professional athletes and putting her workout money where her mouth is.

"Well, I hope you counter-woo your prospects successfully. Any player would be lucky to have you on their coaching team."

She grins. "Okay, okay, enough with the ass kissing. Wes, what's your plan here? Lay it out for me."

I throw my hands in the air. "You're looking at the plan. I declined my scholarship for this year and withdrew from the university. I worked my ass off over the summer to get fit for this weekend and I intend to leave here with offers."

She furrows her brow and looks at me skeptically. I show her my palms. "Yes, I have a fallback plan. If somehow, I leave here without any interest, I'll play for one of the academy clubs for a year and get my ass to the next open camp and the one after that until I get called up."

"Wesley."

I shake my head. "I know my parents' stance on education. I fully intend to finish my degree once I'm done with my professional career. Which is what your husband did, if I recall. And Uncle Ty. I don't need to tell you there's a limited window when my body can handle being a pro athlete."

She sighs. "No, Wes. You don't need to tell me that. But I still don't approve of your approach to this, doing it in a flame of subterfuge. Your dad was embarrassed to be kept in the dark, kiddo. Why would you do that to him?"

We stare at one another for a few beats. I have no good answers for her except that she isn't there when my parents unleash their anxieties on me. Education is so important to my mom that she can't see why I'd pursue anything until I have a degree under my belt. Her epilepsy prevented her from doing so many things physically and I don't know if she really gets that my body is the thing I'm focused on right now.

But my dad is a fucking artist. Yeah, he has a fine arts degree, but he knows what it means to slip into a trance and just let your body do its thing. It makes me nuts when he insists I put my studies ahead of literally everything else. Soccer *is* my everything.

"I have no good answers for you, Aunt Lucy. I'm 21 years old. I'm not relying on them for rent or cash or tuition. If I thought they'd support me in this, I would have come to them with it. I am sorry I kept you and the uncles in the dark—and Aunt Juniper. I don't know. I guess I never expected you'd stage a mass intervention to get my dad to cool his jets."

She rolls her eyes. "Please. All those men do is intervene with each other to cool their jets. You've dug a bit of a hole for yourself, Wes."

I lean back on the recliner. "I'll dig myself out of it after this weekend when I know more about what's in store."

She bites her lip and looks around. "Well, obviously I can't tell you anything in that regard, but you're a smart kid. You know I'm not the only coach who jumped on a plane this weekend."

I grin, but I know better than to push her for details. "There's a lot of top talent here, eh?"

She stands up and whacks me with her clipboard. "Get some food. Get some rest. Play your ass off tomorrow and plan a good grovel with the family ASAP."

I follow her into the hotel feeling pretty damn good about my choices leading up to this moment.

CHAPTER 8
CARA

"I WANT to see crisp passes out there, ladies. Lots of touches on the ball." Coach Akemi wanders up and down the lines of athletes, staring at our feet as we pass the ball and sprint between cones. We've spent the whole morning focusing on fundamentals, basic skills from my preschool days. "The team that has the best ball control is the team that takes home the gold," Akemi says, as if she can read my mind when I start to question the drill.

I think of my roommates, my fellow midfielders on my college team. We always pair up for these drills and we just know each other's style so well. I barely have to look when Shante, Toni, or Rosalie is across the cones from me. I just know they'll deliver the ball directly to my feet and, like a magnet is attached, I can send it right back where it needs to be.

It's hard for me to imagine building that familiarity from scratch, but I knew that would happen after graduation. There was never a second when I thought I'd stop playing soccer. My whole life has led to this moment, to the consideration for the pro women's soccer league, and someday to the national team. My midfield mamis aren't looking for the same experience. They all have graduate school on the horizon and Rosalie hasn't even looked into recreational soccer near where she's heading in Chicago. I need to create new bonds with new players.

So, I focus on my fundamentals here, with a partner I've never seen before, and remind myself that I'll settle into a team. I *will* get signed after this weekend and I will find a group of middies I click with. I punctuate this thought by stopping the ball with the inside of my foot and pushing it to the outside before chipping it across the lane to my partner, whose name I forget. She smiles and dribbles the ball.

"Looking good, Moreno. Nice work." Coach Akemi tips her chin toward the sideline where an army of assistant coaches furiously take notes on all of our performances. Just when I start to worry we will spend the entirety of the day on passing drills, Coach blows her whistle and tells us to huddle up.

"Coach Pat has been putting together some new rosters based on yesterday's scrimmage performance. They will read off your teams, and that's who you will be with for the rest of today's session."

I edge my way closer to Coach Pat, hoping they've put me on the same team as Jay, so I don't have to shoot at her in the goal today. Sure enough, Coach puts us both on the green team and Jay mimes an excited roar when she hears both our names.

There are 60 of us players, split into four teams, and we

spend the rest of the morning cycling through more fundamental skills before the coaches send us off for lunch. Jay drapes an arm around my shoulder and hands me a cup of water as we make our way toward the cafeteria. "I've had enough first-touch practice to last me the rest of my life, I think," she jokes.

"Just wait until we practice shots on goal later." I elbow her in the side, glad to be forging a friendship outside my college network, with someone else focused on the same goals as me. I'm about to make another joke about the agenda when I hear a voice coming toward us.

"Oh good, the two of you are together. That makes things easier." A fit, white woman with shiny brown hair in a ponytail jogs up beside us and smiles, beckoning for us to step out of the sun into the shade of the tunnel toward lunch. "Can you chat for a minute?"

"Sure." Jay furrows her brow, confused.

"I'm Lucy Moyer, fitness coach for the Pittsburgh Hot Metal." Jay's brow stays furrowed. "I'm new to them this year—I was coaching the men's side before that."

I take a deep breath, attempting to calm my racing heart. A coach from a pro team has just pulled me aside to chat, with a pleasant look on her face. Lucy produces two business cards from a fanny pack and Jay and I each grab one. "The two of you really impressed our scouts yesterday. I flew out here to see for myself."

Jay's eyes fly wide, and she seems to bounce in her cleats.

"Wow," I stammer. "Thank you."

"Thank *you,*" Lucy grins. "We really need more depth in the midfield, especially someone good with set pieces." I think back to the corner kick I took yesterday, that Jay swatted away like it was a slow pitch softball. My frustration must be evident on my face because Lucy says, "I was happy to see a fantastic kick with excellent form, and I was excited to see such solid defense on such a banger. Also, with excellent form." She looks at Jay thoughtfully. "I can tell you really work on your core strength and leg flexibility."

The two of us are beside ourselves. I know I haven't had any preparation for next steps since I wasn't in the draft this past spring. I was so focused on getting here, I didn't think about what to do and I'm unsure how to act when it came to the results. I'm guessing Jay hasn't, either. Lucy gestures at the cards we're each holding like they're made of delicate spider webbing. "My cell is on there. Reach out." With a smile she jogs off toward the striker for the blue team.

"So, that was amazing." Jay shakes her head and holds just the edges of the card, trying to keep from smudging it with sweat, I guess. I'm doing the same.

"Are you a hugger? I need a hug right now."

She nods and I throw my arms around her, both of us jumping up and down and squealing before composing ourselves. "Right. Let's fuel up and kick ass this afternoon."

"Check and check."

I nudge her with my elbow as we wait for our food. "You have to go up against the striker from the blue team today."

Jay grins. "She's got nothing on you, roomie. Me and my flexible hamstrings are ready for her."

Someone's gaze bores into me as I sit down with my food. I look over to see Wes gulping down ice water, his throat working spectacularly as he drinks. He and I feel inevitable, our plan to meet later an exclamation point on an amazing morning. I send him my best smile, which he returns with a wink before he heads back out to the field with the rest of the men.

CHAPTER 9
WES

THE FINAL CAMP WHISTLE BLOWS, and I feel incredible. For a few minutes…before the aches and pains set in and my body screams at me for torturing it for 48 hours. I join the parade of sweaty guys heading toward the training room and am pretty happy to see they've got a lot of help, so nobody has to wait very long.

I sign in and get on a table pretty quickly, telling the trainer that the worst pain is in my lower back. He frowns at the clipboard. "Did you participate in the cool-down stretches after the clinic?" I nod and wince when he sets a hand on my flank.

"I think I took an elbow during the scrimmage."

He hums and lifts up my shirt, nodding. He pokes around for a bit and says, "I'm going to hook you up with some stim for 20 minutes. I assume you've had this treatment before?"

"Ugh." I groan in response, wiggling out of my shirt and tugging my shorts down a few inches to expose my lower back for the sensors. I actually love getting hooked up to the TENS machine, feeling those gentle electric pulses in my muscles. It's the next best thing to a real massage. I moan in relief as the trainer gets me all hooked up. He sets the timer by my head and moves on to the next guy. I close my eyes and think through everything that happened.

I played my ass off this weekend. I took a huge gamble to be here, threw away my final year of college eligibility. After some of the conversations I had with the staff here, I'm feeling confident it all worked out. I haven't gotten any official calls yet, but I would expect those to filter in tomorrow morning after the scouts spend this evening unloading to their coaching teams across the country. Hell, maybe even across the world if the rumors are true that some scouts from the UK were watching today.

The stim machine gives me a jolt in a good spot, and I let out a moan before I can help myself. I open my eyes to see most of the guys have filtered out of the training room and the women's team is starting to file in as their session wraps up. My eyes connect with Cara's where she's seated on a table a few down from me while a trainer wraps bags of ice around her shins.

I give her a lazy smile. I am tempted to imagine her hands on my lower back, but I don't want to be sprouting wood here in the training room. That's for later, in private. Ideally with her, if she's still game.

She gives me a look that assures me she is still ready to celebrate and burn off some adrenaline. I smile wider as she licks her lips. I love that she's got the same priorities as me, the same expectations. We both emphasize our game right now, above our personal relationships. Neither of us is going into this expecting forever. Not at all.

She presses her teeth into her plump bottom lip, and I want to fly off the table and capture her tongue with mine. Her expression shifts like she can tell how turned on I am and her confidence is so damn sexy. I never realized before I saw Cara how hot it is when a woman knows what she wants and knows damn well how to get it.

I'm not talking about sex, although her openness about that is hot, too. Cara Moreno can play fucking soccer. She's like me, knowing in her tendons that she's one of the best in the world, capable of competing on the professional stage. There is nothing like that.

I'm glad I got to see her play from afar yesterday, got to see her skill on the field. She's a stunning, incomparable player and I cannot wait for her to direct all those physical strengths toward me.

The tension slips out of my muscles, both because of the treatment and because I'm imagining her straddling me on my bed, me lying back as she does the work to bring us both over the goal line.

The trainer pats Cara on the knee and moves on to the next athlete. Cara hops off the table and takes her time getting her bag. I've been in that place before: she'll wear the bags of ice on her legs until we reach the hotel and then she'll be all set. She bends over to fuss with the zippers, giving me an eye-level show that includes her entire, perfect ass just a few feet from my face. She is absolutely doing that on purpose.

The room is nearly empty now, just a few other athletes and one trainer remaining. Cara approaches my table and her hand trails along my leg, fingers tickling the hairs on my calf, the back of my knee, and fuck! She just keeps on going.

The timer beeps and I yelp, causing Cara to giggle. I struggle to sit up and shout over my shoulder, "Hey, is it ok if I disconnect myself?"

The trainer is stretching a woman's hamstring and glances over at me. "You think you can get all the stickers? Maybe your friend can help you out?"

Cara grins and nods, hands coming to my lower back. Her touch sends stronger shock waves through my body than the machine as she peels off the sticky circles. Her breath is hot against my ear as she says, "I know that stings. I'll kiss it later."

"Later? Fuck that. We're getting out of here immediately."

She giggles again and yanks off the final sticker, patting my back afterward to ease the sting. "I have to eat first. I'm starving."

I run a finger down the side of her neck, watching her shiver a bit as she continues to rub her palm on my back. "I've got something I can feed you, Moreno."

She smacks me and backs up, arching a brow and looking murderous. "I'm serious, Stag. I need protein. Do not make another joke."

I laugh and tug my t-shirt over my head. "I was going to tell you we can order room service. I don't know what you were thinking."

She bites her lip. "What about your roommate?"

I furrow my brow at her. "You have a roommate?"

"You don't have a roommate?" I shake my head and

toss her a protein bar from my bag. "I can't believe the men don't have to share rooms. Fuck you."

I place a hand on her lower back, steering her out of the room and toward the last remaining shuttle bus. "Please do, Cara."

CHAPTER 10
CARA

WES and I are among the last people to leave the stadium, so we have the shuttle bus practically to ourselves. Practically, but not entirely. It's really unlike me to get physical with an audience, but I can't seem to help myself with Wes.

I'm relieved he doesn't have a roommate, that we can go back to his room and not mine. Not only because it would be awkward to navigate all that with Jay, but because I like that I can leave if I want to. I'm not here to get attached. I can't risk the mental distraction, especially if Coach Lucy comes through and I get an offer after this weekend. I can afford to distract myself for a few hours, but then I need to get serious about my future as a professional athlete.

And *then* I need to explain it all to my family, who still thinks I'm playing for fun on the side and doesn't seem to grasp that soccer is what paid for my college education.

But first, Wes Stag.

He guides me to the back seat of the bus and his hand

is on my thigh before his butt hits the seat. He nudges the side of my neck with his nose as he whispers, "Is this okay?"

"God, yes." I choke out the words in a whisper, trying to keep my head facing forward. There are a handful of staff members in the front rows, conversing, and two other players seated not far behind the staff.

I turn my head to look at Wes and want to drown in the dark pools of his eyes. His pupils are totally blown and I know mine are the same. I want him. I want him for his body, I want him because I feel so fucking horny after the work of the weekend. I want him because I want to roar and feel so god damned good celebrating this milestone in my life. I have wanted this for so. Long.

And so has Wes. There is so much unspoken understanding between us, and I want that, too.

His fingers rub my thigh, feeling so good and warm on my screaming muscles. "Everyone else is probably in the pool right now," I whisper.

"Everyone else doesn't have a sexy woman in their arms."

I laugh, thinking of Jay. "My roommate might."

"Good for her." His voice is low, almost a growl. He looks hot as fuck all disheveled from playing, all relaxed from the stim on his lower back. We both smell like sweat and I know if I licked him now, I'd taste the salt of his exertion on his skin. The thought of it should gross me out, but it turns me on even more. I memorize the expression on his face right now, wanting to remember everything about tonight. How I feel as an athlete and how I feel as the woman Wes Stag desires.

The bus hisses to a stop outside the hotel and Wes

grabs both our duffel bags in one hand, my hand in his other as he tugs me down the aisle and into the lobby. I rip the bags of ice off my legs and toss them in the trash as we walk through the hall. He summons the elevator with a knuckle and the second it arrives, I'm flat against the back wall, his arms around me. His chest is pressed against mine and I can feel every hard inch of the body he works so hard to perfect.

"Did you like watching me get an electronic back massage, Cara?"

I nod. His face is so close to mine. I could stick my tongue out and taste him, but the anticipation is almost as hot as I know kissing him will be. "I could watch you do anything." He pulls me even tighter against him and I feel a bulge in his shorts. I never anticipated this—electrifying attraction. The intensity of it. I wonder what he's thinking, but I don't have to guess for long because the elevator dings and Wes pushes off the wall, nodding his head toward the door as he backs out of the small space.

"Come watch me adore you, then."

I follow him down the hall, my cheeks hurting from smiling. Wes drops our bags outside his hotel door but has to root around for his key. I step up behind him and my palms go to his ass before I can think better of it. It's like he bent over right there to taunt me with his soccer glutes. "My god, you're firm," I mutter, giving him a squeeze as he grunts and straightens.

The door opens and he pulls me inside. I squeal as he pushes me against the wall.

He brushes the sweaty hair from my face with one gentle hand and then finally presses his mouth against mine. It's not just a kiss. It's a searing celebration.

His hands press into my sides as his lips move against mine and I sneak my tongue into his mouth with a sigh. It's good between us, hot and aggressive—we both grunt in satisfaction as our bodies fuse together.

Wes pulls back a bit, nibbles at my bottom lip. "What do you think about starting off in the shower?" He sniffs the air, a bit musty from our combined physical exertion.

"Mm," I nod and lick his neck, reveling in the purring sound he makes as I do. "I like that idea, Mr. Stag."

CHAPTER 11
WES

I WANTED her the second she yelled at me at that airport, but now as my eyes dip to her lips, I might catch fire if I don't kiss her. She tastes like trouble, and for a minute I worry that sex with Cara will be too much. I have too much on the line to get attached, and Cara Moreno is the kind of woman I'd want to lock down.

I shake my head. I don't do those things. I don't enter into long-term relationships with women, and I don't incorporate emotions into my weekend flings. We kiss against the wall of my hotel room and all thoughts flee my mind as I open my eyes to see her looking satisfied and starving all at once. I like that I am bringing her what she needs and also leaving her hungry for more. She's horny as fuck for me, and I like how that feels. I like it very much.

When a whiff of my own armpit distracts me, I suggest we start our adventures with a shower. I should have thought of this sooner. My hands fist in her jersey, feeling the silky material under my rough hands. "Take it off," she says, reaching for the hem of my own shirt. I slide hers over her head and move to touch her bra but she shakes her head.

She steps back and her hands go to the elastic band at the bottom of the bra. "This will be wet and gross."

I slip my jersey off quickly so I can watch her wrestle out of her bra. I soak in the view as her tits spring out of the stretchy fabric—perky, golden globes with red-brown nipples standing stiff, calling to me.

"Fuck, Cara." My palms press against those beautiful nubs, rubbing and skittering as she sucks in jagged breath. "I could take you right here, against this wall. You're so fucking sexy, all firm and quivering for me right now." I thrust my hips against hers.

"Please, Wes," she begs, but she doesn't know what she's asking for. Not yet.

"Shower," I grunt, and pull myself back from her. I watch as her knees almost give out, and realizing this strong, powerful woman is literally weak for me is hotter than anything else.

I trip into the bathroom and crank on the shower, yanking down my shorts and briefs in one tug as Cara steps into the room. We both still have our socks on and we each hop around a bit trying to peel them off.

If I'm honest, I've never done this before, undressed from my kit in front of a woman. I've gotten a BJ after a game before, but that didn't involve the sort of intimacy I'm finding in watching Cara pull her sock off her toes. I moan as each red-tipped digit appears, and I know that after we shower, I'm going to kiss her feet. That's a first for me, too.

When did I last feel this way? So free? I've had a

constant struggle over the years with the pressure of elite sports, and I've loved every second of it. But there's something about this woman that lets me relax, puts the stress of all that to the side. How did I just find Cara Moreno now, on a flight to my future?

I test the temperature of the water and gesture for Cara to climb in the shower, where I get my first look at her completely naked. I trace a hand down her side, murmuring to her that she's fucking incredible. Her fingertips trace my abs, running along the line of muscle on my thigh.

It's hot as a fever in the shower and I want to explode at the sight of her dripping wet, beads of water sliding down her gorgeous body. She presses me against the shower wall and grinds against me, slippery and warm, supple, and so fucking firm.

She reaches for the bar of soap and rubs it between her palms, setting it back in the soap dish before working her hands into a lather. And then she runs those foamy hands down my chest, down my stomach. I suck in a breath, hoping she's going to reach for my shaft, but she chuckles and starts soaping up my thighs instead.

"You're cruel," I growl, reaching for the soap. "Two can play at this game." I wash her upper arms as she scrubs my chest. She arches a brow at me, soaping up my back and my ass cheeks while I skip over her boobs and palm her butt.

Finally, with a wicked grin on her face, she slides a soapy palm around my cock, taking me in her hot hand and stroking me from base to tip. I watch her looking at my length in her hand, loving the "mm" sound she makes as she rubs against me.

I reward her by tracing a thumb from her naval down to the neatly trimmed triangle of hair that points toward her clit. It's like an arrow, guiding me toward the prize and she gasps when I reach the destination. "You like that?"

She responds by yanking my shoulders forward, slamming her mouth into mine. Her tongue mimics the motion of my thumb as I slowly stroke along her seam. She's wet and slippery. Warm and inviting me in.

Cara suddenly drops to her knees in the tub, her hands tracing through the hair on my thighs as her tongue snakes out and circles the tip of my cock. "Fuck, Cara, wait."

She pulls her head back, confused. I know if she puts those pouty lips around my dick I'll explode in her mouth in seconds, and I'm just getting started here. I hoist her to her feet again and shake my head, dropping to my knees in front of her instead.

CHAPTER 12
CARA

"FUCK, CARA." That's exactly how I feel, what I want to do right now. I don't want to make love to him. I don't want to have sex. I want to *fuck* this man who just inexplicably stopped me from going down on him in the shower.

I was here, ready to put that delicious cock right into my mouth when he hauled me back to my feet and pressed my back against the tile.

When he sinks to his knees in front of me, I have to grip the soap dish to steady myself as I realize what he plans to do.

I've never had a man excited to go down on me, certainly not like this. Wes looks up with hunger in his eyes as he sticks out his tongue and licks along my core. The sound that comes out of me is obscene, but I don't have time to worry about it as he slides fingers through my wetness. There is nothing selfish about Wesley Stag, not in the bedroom department.

My soreness melts from my consciousness as he licks and strokes, his eyes boring into mine all the while. My head sinks back to the wall and one hand drops to his wet, dark hair as he teases, chuckling, driving me mad with want.

I breathe out, "Oh god, yes, Wes. Fuck. Fuck, that's good." He rubs a cheek against my thigh, his skin just a little bit scratchy with incoming stubble. When he finally touches my clit again with his tongue, the pleasure starts to circulate inside my belly, inside my spine. It radiates down my legs the more he touches and licks. As Wes strokes my pussy, everything goes fuzzy until I finally come in an explosion, screaming and writhing in the shower.

I'm still trembling and moaning as Wes stands up, holding me close and rubbing my back. "I've got you, baby. That was so beautiful. You're perfect when you come for me. God, you taste good."

I lean against him, unable to function in the aftermath of a destructive orgasm, and then I realize he's gently soaping my hair. His fingers massage my scalp as he mutters about how fucking good I taste, how delicious it was when I came on his tongue.

I tip my head up to look at him, blinking as the shampoo stings my eyes. Wes gently guides my head toward the shower spray, rinsing me as I come back into my body.

As I return to consciousness, I reach for him, rock hard beneath my hand. His erection stands almost upright against his stomach, pointing at my bellybutton. Going down on me turned him on, and that realization weakens my knees even more.

I go with the urge and sink to the shower floor, grinning up at him as he grips the wall and swallows. Fuck, his throat is sexy. I grab hold of his length and lick a bead of pre-cum from the tip, enjoying the low moan Wes releases when I do. I circle his tip with the tip of my tongue, then the flat of it, and then I make eye contact with him as I slide him inside my mouth.

He tastes salty, tangy, but clean since we've been in the shower for god knows how long by now. My tongue circles the head of his cock, and he releases an anguished cry. "Fuck, Cara, I want to watch you do that. You're so fucking beautiful with my cock in between those lips of yours, but I want to come inside you."

I shrug and kiss the tip of him, making my way back up to my feet and reaching behind me to shut off the water. "By the way…" I reach for the towel he grabs from the rack on the wall. "I get tested all the time for soccer. I'm healthy. I should have said that before…"

He grins, grabbing his own towel and briskly scrubbing himself dry. "I'm healthy, too."

And then he hauls me into his arms, bride-style, striding from the bathroom and flinging me onto the giant bed. He dives on top of me and stretches an arm to the night stand. "I took advantage of the 'health bin' in the training room yesterday."

I look into his drawer and laugh at the handful of colored condom wrappers and packets of lube. "I didn't know there was a health bin."

He nods, settling himself between my legs, which I gladly wrap around his waist. "We're hot athletes. They know we're going to fuck each other."

"Are you going to fuck me, though? Because I only had one orgasm so far and you're just talking and talking here…"

"Were you expecting two?" He arches a brow and my eyes fly wide before he bursts out laughing. "Because I'm giving you at least three, Cara. Mark my fucking words."

Wes grabs one of the packets of lube and bites open the end, drizzling it along my chest and giving me a look that's absolutely filthy. I realize it's a warming lube as an amazing heat spreads with the liquid. My boobs are shiny and slick, and he adjusts his body so his cock is lined up with my chest. "Push your tits together, Cara."

I comply, watching as his cock disappears between them. He puts one hand on the headboard and the other by my face as he begins to slide in and out of my slicked-up boobs. The tip of his cock appears and I tilt my head to lick it, which makes him gasp. I start to rub my nipples with my thumbs as he moves, the sight both lewd and incredibly sexy. I'm deeply turned on and my arousal starts to drip down my legs. "Wes," I gasp, and he pulls out of my chest, reaching for his pleasure stash and coming up with a foil packet.

"Is this still okay, Cara? Do you still want to do this?"

I nod, words escaping me as I stare at him.

"You have to say it, babe. I need an enthusiastic yes."

"Yes, damn it, Wes. Please fuck me right the hell now."

He grins and settles back between my legs, one hand guiding his hardness right where I need it most. He slides inside, praising me for being so wet, which sends another gush of moisture right to my core.

His chest sinks down to mine, and the lube heats up even more as our bodies slide together. "Wes." All I can do is moan and repeat his name as he fills me. The hand that was guiding his cock returns to my clit and gently rubs as he strokes in and out of my body.

The pressure is perfect and I dig my heels into his butt, thrusting up to meet him, savoring the stretch of him sinking inside me fully. "You feel so good, Wes." He kisses me and pulls out, leaving me empty, on the edge of an orgasm. "You fucking tease." I swat at him and he sinks back in, hard.

My breath leaves me in a grunt as he smiles. "There she is. That's it, Cara." He puts his thumb back on my clit, his palm holding my hips down against the bed as he pounds into me. I come again, harder than the first time, thrashing on the bed and loving the weight of him on top of me, the pressure of him holding my hips still while he continues to roll his own. I pulse around him, sensing every inch of his heat. "Two down, babe."

Wes pulls out abruptly and cups my cheek. "Can you be on top? I want to watch you ride me."

I nod and he flips onto his back, tugging me up and onto his body. I reach for his cock and slide on, bracing my palms against his chest while I adjust to the angle, the fullness.

"Christ, Cara, look at us." He stares down between my legs, watching his cock slide in and out of my body, studying my body stretched around his, swallowing him, welcoming him in. We both watch as I tilt my body and ride him, leaning forward until I know I found the friction I need to come a third time. My eyes widen as it builds. "That's it, baby. Let it happen. Good girl."

And with those words, I fall apart. I tighten my body and release all the pleasure I have and then a secret store of it I wasn't aware of. It floods out of me as I writhe and moan on top of Wes. I come with him deep inside me and he follows, grunting and shouting my name until I collapse onto his chest, panting.

That was the best sex of my life.

"I agree," he says, his voice low and his words slow. I hadn't realized I said that out loud, but I don't regret it.

"Come here," he says, sliding out of me, and tugging off the condom. He tosses it into the trash can by the bed and then pulls me into his arms. He looks at me like I discovered fire. And maybe I did—maybe this spark between us engulfed the entire world while we were in here. I have no idea and no desire to leave this bed to find out.

Wes wraps his arms around me and I'm so secure.

This doesn't make sense. I should be climbing off the bed, gathering my things, and sneaking out of his room. This is a one-night stand, but it feels like so much more. I knew what I wanted when I came up here, but this was … something else.

I know it's ridiculous, but what we just did has changed me.

I look up at him as he runs his fingers through my damp hair and then he kisses the top of my head. "Want me to order up some food?"

"God, yes, please."

CHAPTER 13
CARA

WES ORDERS practically the entire room service menu. We can relax our eating plans a bit now that we've finished the training camp, so we gorge on bread and pasta, making jokes about the meatballs.

"I've never eaten spaghetti naked before," I admit, sitting cross-legged on the bed where he just blew my mind.

"Same, honestly. But it's kind of fun." He winks as he slurps in a long noodle and I shove his shoulder.

"Of course you can wink." I take another bite of food.

"You can't wink?" He gestures at me with a breadstick, and I reach for it, laughing when he snatches it back. "You can't have my stick if you can't wink, Cara. It's a rule."

"I'd like to see this rule in the handbook, please." I snatch the stick from his hands and he laughs, reaching for a napkin.

We finish the food and Wes sets the room service tray on the table next to the bed. His room is pretty small, but the fact that he has it all to himself shows me how wide the chasm still is between men's and women's professional soccer. I don't want to think about that now, though.

I lean back on the bed on my forearms, admiring the look of him, naked and satisfied, his hair messed up from rolling around with it all wet. I wiggle my toes as Wes settles himself on the pillows and then reaches for one of my feet.

"What are you doing—oh, god." He starts to rub my foot, his thumbs pressing along my arch, knuckles pushing against the ball and heel. "Where the fuck did you learn how to do this? Holy shit, Wes." I lean back, knowing I'm ruined for all other men for eternity now that I have had a naked foot massage from Wesley Stag. "Gooodddddd."

"If I had known you'd make those sounds and that expression on your face, I'd have led with this," he says, switching to my other foot.

I want to tell him that would have been gross because my feet would still have been sweaty from my cleats, but I lose all ability to form words when his tongue slides along the sole of my foot. He groans as he slides his lips to my toes, kissing the tips and then easing them into his mouth one at a time, sucking gently. It's very, very sexy and like nothing I've ever experienced before.

"Fuck, Wes. Please keep doing that."

He groans and complies, changing to my other foot before I open my eyes and see him practically unhinged with want. His cock is rock hard again, bobbing against the dark hair on his stomach as he strokes my foot. Wes tugs gently, pulling me closer until my feet are flat against his chest and my core is flush against his straining cock.

He keeps eye contact with me as one hand rubs my foot and the other dips between my legs, stroking. I purr as he slides a finger inside me, then another. Since when do I purr? "That's it, Cara. Does this feel good?" I nod as he switches to the other foot, his left hand now cupping my sex. His thumb presses against my clit, already an expert at the pressure and rhythm I need. I gasp and clench when his index finger traces along my body back to my ass and he grins as he lightly traces the puckered skin there.

"Another time, maybe," he says, turning his head to kiss the bottom of my foot. He keeps his thumb pressed against my clit and continues rubbing my foot until I'm gasping and coming apart for a fourth time, awash in new sensations.

When I can think again, I yank my foot from his hand and haul myself to my knees, crawling up the bed toward his cock like a jungle cat stalking a meal. He lets me take him into my mouth, sighing and settling back on the pillows as I give his rod the same treatment he just gave my feet and my pussy combined. Wes drops a reverent hand to my cheek as I slide him to the back of my throat. It's not long before he groans and stiffens. His abs contract and he gasps, as if startled by the intensity of his orgasm. Wes shudders and spurts into my mouth, and then he groans again as I swallow every drop.

He falls asleep soon after and I cuddle up against him, turning off the light and allowing myself to sink into the cocoon of his arms while my brain cranks into overdrive. I think about the weekend, about how I played. I'm confident I put my best self forward at this camp, on the pitch and in this bed. I blush, remembering Wesley's curious finger on my ass. The two of us could create something explosive together, but then I remember we came here with a specific mission.

Our game is important to us. I have no idea where I'll wind up after tomorrow, and he could go anywhere as well—rumor had it there were scouts from Europe here to see the men playing. My thoughts drift to the national team, knowing that's no longer a pipe dream but a real possibility for me in the years to come.

For one instant, I remember the uncomfortable way the Soccer USA president made me feel in the stadium before Jay called my name. Before I can dwell on that moment, Wes pulls his arm tighter around me. I drift off to sleep in his embrace.

My eyes fly open before dawn. The light shining behind the curtains is purple, like the sun hasn't quite made up its mind whether to rise. *What am I doing?*

The whole point of doing this in Wes's room was that I could leave, head back to my room and get a proper rest before my long flight home. I cannot get attached to orgasms and foot rubs. I have to focus, keep my eye on my goals.

I slip out of bed slowly, but Wes is out to the world. My body aches from the long weekend of too much exercise, and my crotch aches from the dick I rode last night. But I ignore the slight sting. As quietly as I can, I gather up my things and use the light of my phone to dig out a clean-ish change of clothes from my soccer bag, thankful I don't have to squeeze myself back into the disgusting post-workout clothes from yesterday.

I slip out of Wes Stag's room for a walk of shame. Except, I don't feel very shameful. I feel pretty incredible and I smile as I weave through the hall. I call the elevator and grin when I see Coach Lucy Moyer inside.

"Oh my god, it's you! I was just coming to slide a note under your hotel door."

"Seriously?"

She nods, thrusting a piece of paper into my hands. "I want you to have your agent call this number as soon as possible," she says, tapping a number highlighted in bright yellow. "You're going to get multiple offers today and I'd like Pittsburgh to be part of that conversation."

The elevator door shoves against Lucy's sneaker, and she gestures me inside the car. "I, uh, don't have an agent." I bite my lip and then grimace. There's so much I'm unprepared for. So much. A further reminder of why I can't lose my head in a man, no matter how many orgasms he hands out in one night. A boyfriend won't get me where I need to be professionally.

Lucy grins and unzips her fanny pack with a flourish. She fishes out a card and hands it to me. "I want you to call this number immediately, then." I look at the card. Lucy continues. "Don't worry about the time or day. This woman is fair and fierce. Call her." The elevator door slides open, and I see we've gone down to the lobby.

Lucy gives me a small push. "I have to go hunt down two more prospects, Cara, but call that number." She mimes punching numbers onto a phone as the elevator door slides shut.

I'm left standing in the lobby with all my dreams in my hand. It felt a little like fate brought me here this weekend to cross paths with Wes Stag, but that's not it at all. He was fun. We go together like smoke and fire. But this is my purpose. This is my future.

CHAPTER 14
WES

I'M ALONE. I'm aware of that reality before I'm fully awake in a room where I should have the gorgeous body of Cara Moreno draped over my chest.

I can't fight the disappointment that simmers, even though I know what last night was to both of us. It was a celebration. Releasing a pressure valve. We both have a lot riding on the camp from this weekend and riding each other was a celebration and a release.

Except, it didn't feel that way to me.

I did things with Cara that I've never done before, never wanted to do. We had a connection and a lump forms in my throat when I realize that was clearly a one-sided assumption. She didn't even leave a note. I reach for my phone to see if maybe she texted me, and it starts ringing in my hand.

Unknown number.

I have to answer it, in case it's an offer, but I'm not prepared for the volume that comes bellowing at me at … I glance at the alarm clock … 6:30.

"Wes! Baby!"

"Hello?"

"Don't you know my voice, kid? That's okay. Listen, your Uncle Hawk told me to give you a ring, said you're going to need me today."

I comb my memories, trying to place the too-chipper voice on the other end of the phone. "Brian?"

"The one and only." My uncle's sports agent starts praising my game, comparing me to the family legacy, whatever that means. I wake up more fully and start to process the meaning of his call.

"Wait. My uncle called you?"

"Damn right he did, and not a minute too soon. The sharks are swimming outside your door, baby."

I glance toward the hotel door and see a bunch of slips of paper on the carpet. Huh.

"Listen," Brian continues. "I'm not going to dance around. You know I was a good partner for your Uncle Hawky and made him a shit-ton of money over the years. I can guarantee you the same treatment the second you sign an agreement with me. I can text it to you, and I can be on the phone with those sharks in the lobby of your hotel within minutes. Where do you want to land, Wesley? Name your team."

I drag a hand through my hair. "Name my team? Seriously?"

He sighs. "Okay, not quite that awesome. But give me a ranked list. Word on the street is that your debut will be electric."

If my uncle called his agent, that means Aunt Lucy wasn't kidding when she hinted that my "subterfuge" worked in my favor. My stomach flutters and I stand up, pacing the floor. I catch a glimpse of myself in the mirror, with obvious sex-tousled hair, swollen lips, and scratch marks on my chest. Cara sticking around to celebrate would feel too good to be true. Last night she made me feel like I can do anything, achieve anything I want.

This morning, it's all happening ... but she's not here. I sigh as Brian talks about numbers and sponsorship plans. It all sounds great, actually. So maybe it was better to have one perfect night than keep things going, grow frustrated with one another as we dive headfirst into intense schedules and camera shoots and too much travel. That's no way to kick off a relationship.

"Sounds amazing, Brian. Text me the thing to sign."

A pang of sadness stings me—my dad isn't here with me when I sign my first contract with an agent. I'll most likely be signing with a pro team in a few hours without my family celebrating. My Aunt Alice would have made a grain-free cake out of vegetables or some shit. My cousins would have gotten kazoos and done a damn parade around the Highland Park fountain if I'd looped them in.

Or they wouldn't have done anything, because my mom would have cried, and my dad would have glowered at me and I would have stayed in school another year and blown my ACL. I can't grieve what didn't happen any more than I can regret my choices.

Brian texts me an agreement and I sign it with my thumb on my cell phone, alone in a dark hotel room.

A few seconds later, Brian texts me instructions to head down to the lobby in twenty minutes, and he'll video chat with me while I have a conference with an offer. And there it is: my new life...the one I planned for. The one I set in motion.

I should want to call my cousins, or the guys from my college team, but the first person I think of is Cara. Did she get a similar offer this morning? Should I find her room and go another round with her to celebrate, real quick before we both fly out? Does she have an agent? Maybe I should send her Brian's contact info…

These thoughts swirl in my mind as I brush my teeth and slip into the only clean clothes I have left: sweats and an old Pittsburgh Forge t-shirt of my Uncle's.

I step out of the elevator on the ground floor and turn the corner, toward the conference rooms. Toward my new life.

CHAPTER 15
CARA

I STAGGER over to a column around the corner in a quiet hallway, staring down at the card and the offer note from the Pittsburgh Hot Metal. Is this really my life? I have a fleeting thought again that I should run back up to Wes's room and tell him, but that's too much. He was pretty clear that he's not looking for long term.

But damn it, we shared something powerful. And I know he'd want to celebrate this moment with me. With my future squared away, maybe it is possible that I can think about something romantic, too. With the right guy it could work—and Wes Stag would definitely understand that soccer would be my top priority, that I'd be flying all over the country and spending long hours at the stadium studying the game.

Maybe we won't have time to be each other's everything, but maybe we can also be something. Somehow. If I can rise above my doubts and make a splash to the pro soccer coaches, surely I can maintain some sort of meaningful friendship … with benefits?

I take a moment to experience some of the joy bubbling inside me, squeaking and bouncing on my toes, letting my duffel bag fall to the ground and then freezing when it makes a loud sound in the echoey space. A man pokes his head around the corner from a conference room and I cringe a little inside when I see it's the Lou-guy who creeped me out in the tunnel the other day. "Hey there," he drawls, and I force a smile onto my face. He's wearing a Soccer USA polo again and I am fairly confident he's someone important with the national team staff.

"Hi," I mutter, folding my note from Lucy and stooping to get my bag. When I stand up, I realize Lou is in my personal space again, one arm on the column and the other reaching for my bag. Stunned, I hand it over to him and he drops it to the floor again.

Every muscle in my body tenses as he smiles a weird, creepy grin. I can't quantify my feelings, but I know he's not interested in my soccer skills. *He's a predator.* The thought frightens me because I know he shouldn't be—he is a man in power in a world I'm trying to access. Every neuron in my brain is panicking but I also know that I can't just dart away because, well, I fucking came here to be seen by the national team. And that's this guy, apparently.

"Did I see you talking with Lucy Moyer yesterday?" I nod, trying to avoid eye contact. He leans in a little closer, his voice near my ear in a whisper. "I'm so glad. I've had my eye on you, Cara Moreno. I think we can expect big things."

My voice cracks as I frantically try to respond in a way that might satisfy this guy while somehow also communicating that I do not like this type of attention. "Thank you,

Mr. Rubeo." Everything I have is clenched right now, my arms stiff and frozen in place, my feet cemented to the tile floor. My breath comes in rapid bursts. "I, um, really need to go meet with Coach Moyer..."

He nods but doesn't back out of my space, his mouth still twisted in a lewd smile that will haunt my dreams. "You do that, Ms. Moreno. We want to make sure you are all squared away on the right track." He traces one finger along my shoulder with his final word of that sentence, tapping the top of my arm before turning around and finally, blessedly, stepping back.

The air returns to my lungs in a whoosh as he takes another step further from me, saying, "Ah. Mr. Stag! Glad I caught you in time."

And then I see Wes in the hall, staring, face twisted in confusion. His eyes bore into mine as Rubeo drapes an arm around Wes's shoulder, guiding him toward the conference room. Wes turns his head back to face me one final time, his expression pained, before he closes his eyes, swallows, and faces Rubeo with stoicism.

As they step into the conference room and shut the door, I fear every possibility I might have had with Wesley Stag is gone.

Don't worry! Wes and Cara's story continues in Forging Glory: Stag Generations Book 1, coming soon wherever books are sold. (Turn the page to read a sneak peek...)

Can't wait for release day? Check out Wes's Uncle Hawk and Aunt Lucy's story, Beautiful Game!

FORGING GLORY EXCERPT

WES

I should consider myself lucky. I should be over the moon excited because all my damn dreams came true. I drop my bag on the floor of my new apartment and it just sounds empty, a cracking thud in an echo chamber since none of my stuff has been moved over yet.

I've been back in my hometown for a month and my parents are still giving me the cold shoulder, which means Stag family gatherings are downright awkward. I never dared to hope that the pro team who signed me would be the one right in my backyard, where my cousins and aunts and uncles all live as one giant family. And here I am, back in the herd…except not really.

I drag a hand through my hair, wondering again how these things still bother me so much when I'm an adult, with my own career and now my own place. So what if Sunday dinner at my uncle's house was fraught?

I check my watch. The movers should be here by now. That thought causes another pang of hurt, though. When my cousin Pete moved into his first solo apartment, an army of Stags hauled all his clothes and furniture up three flights of stairs in about a half hour. And then we all unpacked his kitchen and Aunt Alice made dinner to break in the place.

It doesn't feel like my choices should warrant such a big rift that I don't even get my brother here to help me, but everyone's on pins and needles because my dad, notoriously grouchy glass artist Thatcher Stag, and my mom, A-list author Emma Stag, are pissed that I left college to play professional soccer. It felt a little deliberate that Dad announced a new gallery opening taking place the same day I told them I was moving into my condo.

I wish Brian, my agent, had gotten me a contract with a team a little further from home. Just my luck, the Pittsburgh Forge fought for me and I'm spending 80 hours a week with my Uncle Hawk as my head coach. Hawk can apparently compartmentalize, treating me like one of the guys on the field and flinching when I talk to him outside the stadium.

The elevator bings from the hall and I sigh, a little relieved that the movers will distract me from my sorry state. I try to stay out of their way as they unload my crappy yard-sale furniture and hand-me-down kitchen stuff. It definitely looks out of place in the swank industrial loft I bought from our family friends. Mom's best friend Maddie and her husband decided they wanted a place with a yard after raising their kids in the Strip District. It doesn't make sense to me, but I was happy to get a deal on a two-bedroom.

As a brand new pro rookie, I'm not pulling in *fuck-you-money* yet, but I should be able to do better than an Ikea couch and an ancient wingback chair. I'll add the furniture to the list of things that make me feel inadequate right now, I guess.

I hear more footsteps echoing in the hall and furrow my brow. How many movers did I hire?

"Yo, cuz, you home?" My ears perk up at the sound of my cousin Odin. When I stick my head out the door I'm relieved to see Odin alongside his brothers, all four of them grinning in loosened ties and unbuttoned collars.

"Did you ditch my dad's event to come here?"

Gunnar shrugs and drapes his suit coat over one shoulder. "We put our time in. We stared at the sculptures, we used all the adjectives from our cheat sheet, and we waited five entire minutes after our dad left to sneak out the back door."

"Like four giant Stag kids can *sneak* anywhere." I smile as they pull me in to a group hug. It's a bit like tumbling in a dryer as I nearly drown in their massive shoulders and beefy arms. Their dad, my Uncle Ty, was a pro hockey star and they're built just like him.

Tucker drops his jacket on my shitty couch and walks toward the kitchen, ripping open a cardboard box with his meaty hands. Gunnar and Alder follow suit while Odin heads down to the truck after the movers, returning a few minutes later with a dresser balanced on his back, still wearing his necktie.

I stoop to take the dresser from him, or at least carry the bottom of it, but he grunts at me. "I got it. You get the drawers."

"Come on, dude. Don't be like that." It sounds like he's just being nice, or even just being stubborn about carrying the heavy furniture, but I know there's history at play here. "I'm fine."

Odin growls as he stomps past me and drops the dresser on the floor in the front bedroom. "I know you're fine. I know you're in top shape and everything is perfect." He claps a meaty paw on my shoulder and squeezes. "You're also a lanky soccer dude and I'm a big-ass linebacker. So let me do my thing and then I can look your mom in the eye at family dinner this week."

Alder punctuates this by dropping a frying pan on my stovetop, causing us all to look over at the open kitchen. He shrugs. "You need to clean this thing, dude. The handle's all greasy."

"I'll get right on that."

We all laugh and I give Odin a pass, since all that's left is my bed, and that fucker is heavy as hell. I fall in line with Tucker and Gunnar unwrapping dishes as all of the movers plus Odin stagger in the rolling door with my king-sized bed frame and then the mattress.

One thing my family has always been united about is the value of a good bed. All us Stag men are over six feet tall, and nobody wants to spend their life sleeping diagonally in order to keep their feet supported in their own damn bed at night.

Soon, the movers clear out and another batch of my cousins comes in the front door—my Uncle Tim's kids this time—Pete, Stellan, and Byron. I feel more and more at ease, more hope that things will work themselves out eventually as my cousin Wyatt and his sister Birdy saunter in carrying bags of takeout food.

The labeled containers bear my Aunt Alice's handwriting, and I see that she made a separate container just for me with oatmeal cookies. My aunt is a chef and always knows how to make delicious food that fits inside my nutrition parameters when I'm in season.

I look around my apartment, wondering when the happiness will set in. I've worked for this for 20 years. Why does achieving my goals just make me feel so empty?

I think back to the training camp where I signed my contract, alone with Brian on video chat. That weekend, I opened up to a woman who seemed in sync with me. It felt like we had a powerful connection. And then the next morning I saw that I was fooling myself as much as my parents think I'm fooling myself that my back can withstand the challenge of professional full-contact soccer.

I eat a second cookie and slide the container toward my cousins, trying to ignore the ache in my heart as well as my spine.

Grab Forging Glory to keep reading!

ALSO BY LAINEY DAVIS

Bridges and Bitters series

Fireball: An Enemies to Lovers Romance (Sam and AJ)

Liquid Courage: A Marriage in Crisis Romance (Chloe and Teddy)

Speed Rail: A Single Dad Romance (Piper and Cash)

Last Call: A Marriage of Convenience Romance (Esther and Koa)

Binge the following series in eBook, paperback, or audio!

Brady Family Series

Foundation: A Grouchy Geek Romance (Zack and Nicole)

Suspension: An Opposites Attract Romance (Liam and Maddie)

Inspection: A Silver Fox Romance (Kellen and Elizabeth)

Vibration: An Accidental Roommates Romance (Cal and Logan)

Current: A Secret Baby Romance (Orla and Walt)

Restoration: A Silver Fox Redemption Romance (Mick and Celeste)

Oak Creek Series

The Nerd and the Neighbor (Hunter and Abigail)

The Botanist and the Billionaire (Diana and Asa)

The Midwife and the Money (Archer and Opal)

The Planner and the Player (Fletcher and Thistle)

Stag Brothers Series

Sweet Distraction (Tim and Alice)

Filled Potential (Ty and Juniper)

Fragile Illusion (Thatcher and Emma)

A Stag Family Christmas

Beautiful Game (Hawk and Lucy)

Stag Generations Series

Forging Passion (Wes and Cara prequel)

Forging Glory (Wes and Cara)

Forging Legacy (coming soon)

Forging Chaos (coming soon)

Stone Creek University

Deep in the Pocket: A Football Romance

Hard Edge: A Hockey Romance

Possession: A Football Romance

Made in the USA
Middletown, DE
24 March 2024